XMAS '83

This Book Belongs To

JOANNE

Love
Aunt Margaret
&
Uncle Larry

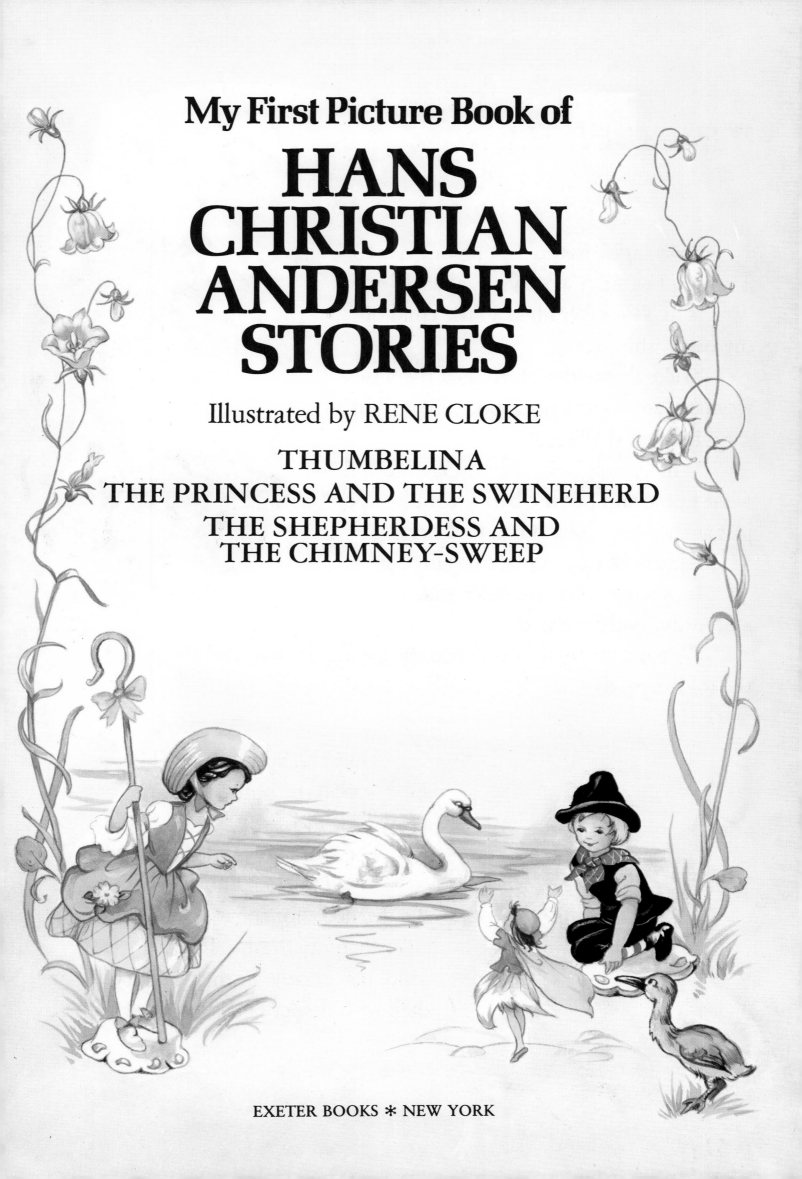

My First Picture Book of
HANS CHRISTIAN ANDERSEN STORIES

Illustrated by RENE CLOKE

THUMBELINA
THE PRINCESS AND THE SWINEHERD
THE SHEPHERDESS AND
THE CHIMNEY-SWEEP

EXETER BOOKS * NEW YORK

THUMBELINA

A young wife was talking one day to a wise old woman who was really a fairy.

"Oh, I do wish I had a little child of my own," she sighed.

"Take this barley corn," said the wise woman, "sow it in a plant pot and you shall see what you shall see!"

"Thank you," said the young wife and she went home and put the barley corn in a pot, just as the wise woman had told her.

Almost at once a plant began to grow.

It became taller and taller and, at last, a beautiful bud appeared.

"What a lovely flower", cried the young woman and she kissed the folded petals

Then the flower opened and there in the centre sat a tiny little girl.

The woman was delighted.

"I will call her Thumbelina," she decided, "for she is scarcely taller than my thumb. I will make her a cradle from a walnut shell with flower petals for sheets."

One night when Thumbelina was asleep, an old toad hopped through the window.

"This pretty little girl would make a good wife for my son," she croaked and, taking the walnut shell cradle, she crawled back to the stream where she lived with her ugly son.

"We will leave her on this water lily leaf," said the mother toad, "while we decorate our home with kingcups and **bullrusles**".

Poor Thumbelina sat on the broad leaf and cried so bitterly that a kind fish gnawed through the stem of the leaf and Thumbelina floated away down the stream where the toads could not follow her.

A white butterfly fluttered by and Thumbelina tied her sash around him and on and on they went together; then a cockchafer picked her up, flew away with her and left her sitting on a daisy.

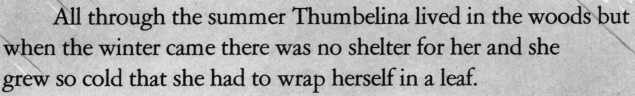

All through the summer Thumbelina lived in the woods but when the winter came there was no shelter for her and she grew so cold that she had to wrap herself in a leaf.

One evening she came to the house of a field mouse at the edge of a corn field and begged a little corn to eat.

"Come in," cried the mouse, "and warm yourself, you poor little thing!"

The field mouse was very kind.

"You may live in my house all the winter," she said, "you can help me to keep it clean and tell me stories; I love to listen to stories."

They lived together very comfortably.

"We are to have a visitor soon," the mouse told Thumbelina one day, "my neighbour, the mole, is calling to see me. He would be a fine husband for you, for his house is much bigger than mine."

But Thumbelina did not like the old mole; he had never seen the sun or the flowers and lived all his life underground.

He told them about a dead bird which lay in one of his tunnels.

"He is a silly swallow who sang and chirped throughout the summer," grumbled the mole, "and now he is starved and frozen."

Thumbelina felt so sorry for the poor bird that she crept out of her bed that night and took a little rug to spread over him.

"Thank you for your songs, dear bird," she whispered and kissed him gently.

To her surprise she found that the bird was not dead after all and soon revived with the warmth of the rug.

Every day she brought him food and water but she didn't tell the mole and the field mouse that he was alive.

The bird soon grew stronger and when the spring came he said good-bye to Thumbelina.

"Fly on my back to the green countryside," he begged her.

"No," said Thumbelina sadly, "the field mouse will be very vexed if I leave her, so good-bye, dear bird, good-bye," and she went back to the little house.

"We must make some pretty clothes for your wedding," said the field mouse, "for you are to marry dear old mole in the autumn."

In the evenings, the mole would listen to Thumbelina's stories, while the field mouse sewed beautiful little dresses for the wedding.

When the autumn came, Thumbelina begged the field mouse to let her wander once more in the fields before she had to live underground.

"Run along, then," said the field mouse kindly, "but don't wander too far."

Thumbelina looked at the blue sky and felt the sun warming her face.

"Tweet – tweet."

There was a fluttering of wings and the swallow flew over her head.

"The winter will soon be here," he chirped, "come with me and I will take you to warm countries away from the old mole and his dark house full of tunnels! You saved my life, now let me help you."

"Yes, yes!" cried Thumbelina and she scrambled on to the swallow's back.

Away they went, over the sea and over snowy mountains, until they came to a land where the sun shone more brightly than Thumbelina had ever seen it.

The swallow came to rest on an old marble pillar in a
lovely garden by the side of a lake and Thumbelina looked
around in delight.

In a beautiful white flower stood
an elf wearing a golden crown.
"I am the king of the fairies,"
he told Thumbelina, "will you be
my queen?"

So Thumbelina became the queen of the fairies and was given many presents; the best of all was a pair of butterfly wings so that she and the fairy king could fly together from flower to flower for evermore.

THE PRINCESS AND THE SWINEHERD

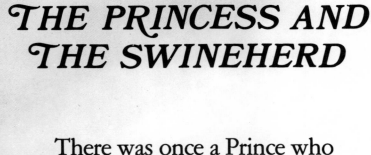

There was once a Prince who
wished to marry a Princess but he
was not rich and all he could give
her was a rose and a nightingale.

He sent these to the palace
in fine caskets and the Princess
clapped her hands in great excitement.

"I wonder if one holds a kitten and the other a musical
box," she cried.

But when she saw the rose and the nightingale she was
disappointed.

"They are both real," she complained, "I wish they were
toy ones."

The Prince, however, was not discouraged; he dressed himself
in old clothes and asked for work at the palace.

"Well," said the King,
"I do need someone to
look after the pigs."

So the Prince
became the Royal
Swineherd.

He sat in the pigsty
and worked away,
making a little
cooking pot with
bells on it.

When it boiled, it played a merry tune
and anyone, who put his finger in the steam,
could smell just what everyone in the town was
having for dinner.

The Princess heard the tune and longed to have the cooking
pot, so her Maid of Honor asked the Swineherd the price of it.
"I want ten kisses from the Princess," the Swineherd told her.
"How tiresome!" said the Princess, "but I must have it. All my
ladies must spread their skirts so that no one can see me."

So the Swineherd got the ten kisses and the Princess and her
ladies had a merry time with the little cooking pot.

The next thing the Swineherd made was a
rattle which played all the tunes in the world.

"How much does he want for it?"
asked the Princess.

"One hundred kisses," answered
the Maid of Honor.

The ladies held out their skirts to hide the Princess but
this time the King was looking out of his window.

"You rascals!" he cried. "Off you go, both of you!"

So the Princess and the Swineherd were banished from the palace.

"I wish I had married the Prince who sent me the rose and the
nightingale." sobbed the Princess.

The Swineherd threw off his rough clothes and appeared in
his princely costume.

"You would not accept a Prince who was poor," he cried, "but
you would give your kisses to a Swineherd for a silly toy. Now,
I despise you."

He went back to his own kingdom and shut his palace door and
the Princess was left crying
in the rain.

THE SHEPHERDESS AND THE CHIMNEY~SWEEP

Two little china figures stood on a table and looked at each other; one was a Shepherdess and one was a Chimney Sweep.

"How beautiful she is," sighed the Chimney Sweep, "her face is so pink and white and her dress is so graceful."

"Although he is a Chimney Sweep," said the Shepherdess, "he is as clean and neat as a Prince."

They loved each other very much and would have been quite happy if it had not been for the Field-Marshal-Major-General-Corporal-Sergeant.

Now this funny person was carved in wood on the front panel of an old fashioned cabinet and the two little china figures were rather afraid of him.

The Chinese Mandarin, who was the grandfather of the Shepherdess, nodded his head. "He will make you a fine husband, he has a whole cabinet of silver!"

"I won't marry him!" declared the Shepherdess, "I don't want to live in a gloomy cabinet."

The Chimney Sweep comforted her.

"We will creep off this table," he whispered, "and go into the wide world. I will work for you, sweeping chimneys."

When the Chinese Mandarin was asleep, they stepped down from the table and ran across the floor.

First they hid in an open drawer where some playing cards were watching a puppet theatre, but the play was very sad and made the Shepherdess cry, so they had to find another hiding place.

"We had better climb up the chimney," said the Chimney Sweep, "that will lead us out to the wide world. I know the way – are you brave enough to come with me?"

"Yes," whispered the Shepherdess.

The Chinese Mandarin woke up and started rocking his head to and fro.

"Quick!" cried the Chimney Sweep, and, taking the Shepherdess by the hand, he hurried to the fireplace.

It was very dark in the chimney but they could see a star shining down through the chimney-pot as they climbed slowly up and up.

At last they reached the roof and sat down to rest, for they were very tired.

The sky above them was full of stars and all the wide world lay beneath them.

"Oh, dear," cried the little Shepherdess, "I'm frightened, the world is too big! I wish I were back on the table again."

The Chimney Sweep reminded her of the Chinese Mandarin and the old Field-Marshal-Major-General-Corporal-Sergeant, but she wept so much that he had to agree to take her back again.

Down the chimney they crept, to the fireplace and into the room.

There, on the floor, lay the Chinese Mandarin broken in pieces, for he had fallen off the table when he had tried to follow the runaways.

"Poor Grandfather, I wonder if he can be mended?" said the Shepherdess.

He *was* mended but a stiff rivet was put in his neck and he could no longer nod his head to and fro.

"Can I have your grand-daughter for my wife?" asked the Field-Marshal-Major-General-Corporal-Sergeant, but the Chinese Mandarin couldn't nod his head, so the two little china figures remained together on the table and loved each other for ever and ever.